5 Wild Creature Adventures!

The editors would like to thank Jim Breheny, Director Bronx Zoo and EVP of WCS Zoos & Aquarium, New York, for his assistance in the preparation of Wild Animal Babies!, Wild Insects and Spiders!, Wild Predators, *and* Wild Reptiles.

The editors would like to thank Paul L. Sieswerda, Aquarium Curator (retired), New York Aquarium, for his assistance in the preparation of Wild Sea Creatures.

Visit us on the Web!
StepIntoReading.com
randomhousekids.com

Educators and librarians, for a variety of teaching tools, visit us at
RHTeachersLibrarians.com

ISBN 978-1-101-93900-0
MANUFACTURED IN CHINA
10 9 8 7 6

Learning to Read, Step by Step!

Ready to Read   Preschool–Kindergarten
• big type and easy words • rhyme and rhythm • picture clues
For children who know the alphabet and are eager to begin reading.

Reading with Help   Preschool–Grade 1
• basic vocabulary • short sentences • simple stories
For children who recognize familiar words and sound out new words with help.

Reading on Your Own   Grades 1–3
• engaging characters • easy-to-follow plots • popular topics
For children who are ready to read on their own.

Reading Paragraphs   Grades 2–3
• challenging vocabulary • short paragraphs • exciting stories
For newly independent readers who read simple sentences with confidence.

Ready for Chapters   Grades 2–4
• chapters • longer paragraphs • full-color art
For children who want to take the plunge into chapter books but still like colorful pictures.

STEP INTO READING® is designed to give every child a successful reading experience. The grade levels are only guides; children will progress through the steps at their own speed, developing confidence in their reading.

Remember, a lifetime love of reading starts with a single step!

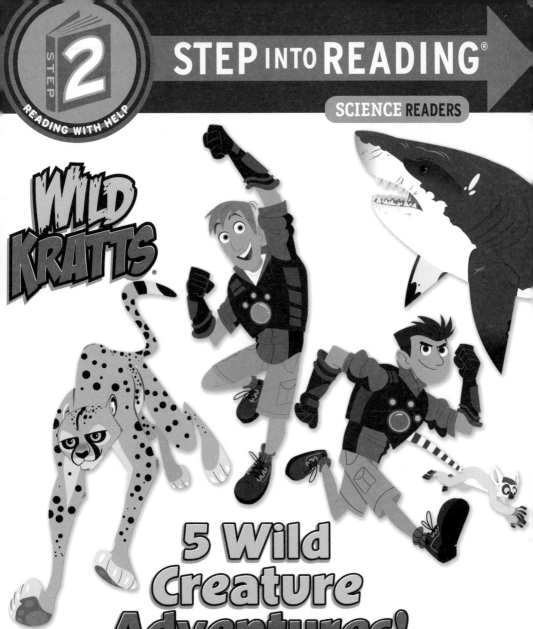

WILD KRATTS

5 Wild Creature Adventures!

Step 2 Books

A Collection of Five Early Readers

by **Martin Kratt and Chris Kratt**

Random House 🏠 New York

Contents

Wild Animal Babies!

by Martin Kratt and Chris Kratt

Random House 🏠 New York

Hey, it's us,
the Kratt Brothers.
I'm Martin.
And I'm Chris.

We love learning about
the Creature Powers
of different animals—
especially baby animals!

Animal babies
aren't just cute.
They play and practice
every day to learn
about their amazing
Creature Powers!

Let's go meet some of our favorite baby animals in the wild!

Giant Pandas!

Stuffo has to learn how to eat bamboo. He practices holding it with a thumb-like pad while he chews.

"Thanks for the hug,
Stuffo," says Martin.

Zebras!

Zebra babies like Maze
are called foals.
Maze was ready to run
on the day she was born.

"And here's why!"

Chris shouts.

"Hungry lions are coming!

Let's get out of here fast!"

Orangutans!

Orangutan babies have
strong feet and hands.
They spend most of
their lives in the trees.
They have to hang on tight.

"You have quite a grip!"
says Chris.

Cheetahs!

Spotswat learns to climb
with his mom
to get a better look around.
Cheetahs watch out
for dinner–and danger!

A cheetah cub's favorite
game is chase!
When Spotswat grows up,
he will have to hunt
for his own dinner.

Sea Otters!

Sea otter pups learn to float when they are very little. Cork can also take a rest on his mom's belly.

Cork is a good swimmer.
His thick fur keeps him
warm in the cold water.

Spider Monkeys!

Grabsy is learning
a special kind of swinging
called brachiation.
She moves hand over hand
through the trees.

Spider monkeys can
swing very fast!
"Go, Grabsy, go!"
shout the brothers.

Wolves!

Howler made his first howl
when he was six weeks old.
Howling helps a wolf pack
talk to each other
and stay together.

Arrrrhooooooo!

"I hear you howling,"
Martin tells Chris.

Ring-Tailed Lemurs!

Clingon rides on
her mom's back
while she is young.
She has to hold on tight.

Mom runs and jumps
from tree to tree.
She takes care of Clingon
until she can survive
on her own.

Our animal friends play
to practice their special
Creature Powers.
What Creature Power
will you practice today?

STEP INTO READING®

STEP 2 READING WITH HELP

A SCIENCE READER

WILD KRATTS

wild Insects and Spiders!

by Martin Kratt and Chris Kratt

Random House 🏠 New York

Hey, it's us,
the Kratt Brothers–
Martin and Chris!
And we love insects
and spiders.

"You mean like the bee on my face?" Martin asks.

"Exactly!" Chris says.

bee

Insects have six legs.
They have three body
parts: a head, a thorax,
and an abdomen.

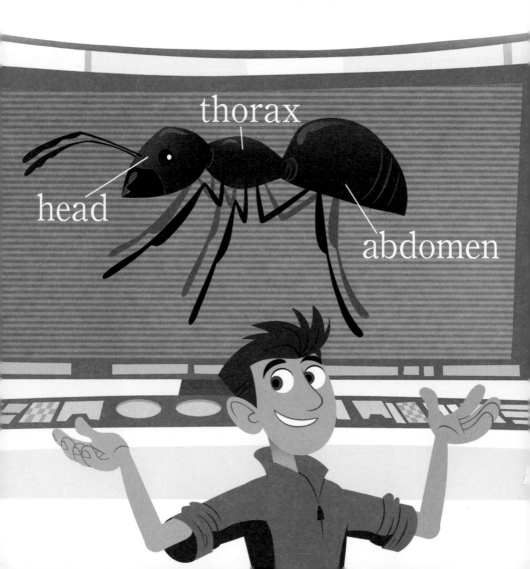

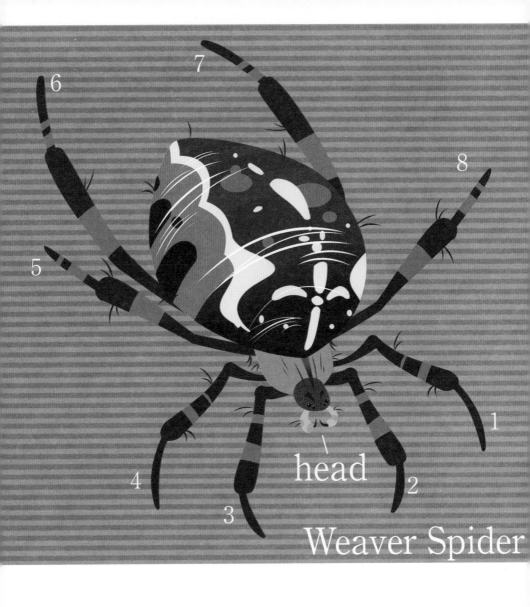

6 7 8 5 1 head 2 4 3

Weaver Spider

Spiders have eight legs.
They are arachnids,
not insects.

Dragonfly!

Dragonflies have been
around since the time
of the dinosaurs.

They can fly forward,
backward, and even
upside down!
"It's a great flying power!"
says Martin.

Dragonflies are predators. They use their flying powers to catch insects right out of the air.

But they can also be prey.
Baby alligators love
to eat dragonflies.
"Watch out!" Chris says.

Mosquito!

Mosquitoes survive by sucking the blood of animals, including humans!

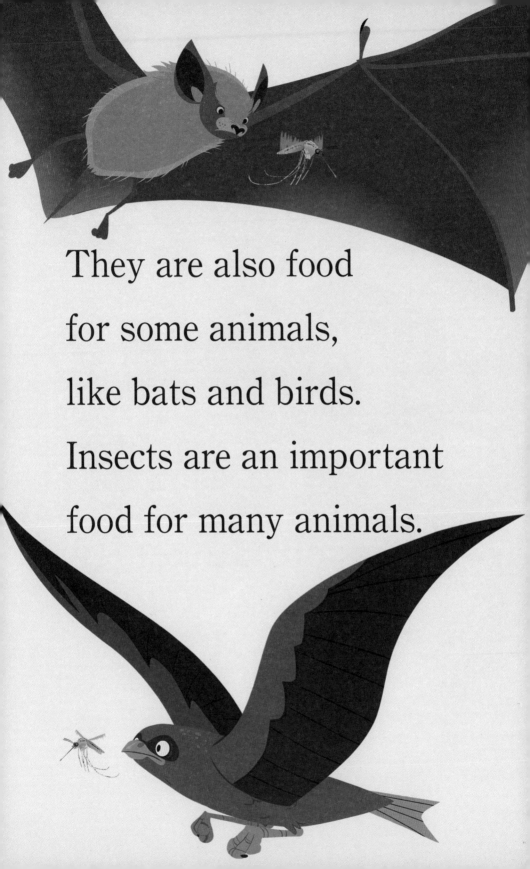

They are also food
for some animals,
like bats and birds.
Insects are an important
food for many animals.

Monarch Butterfly!

Butterflies are strong fliers.
Some can fly
thousands of miles.

But like many insects, they have to crawl before they can fly. "I'm not flying yet," says Martin.

The Butterfly Life Cycle!

First an egg is laid,
and a caterpillar hatches.
After eating lots of leaves,
it makes a cocoon around
itself—the pupa stage.

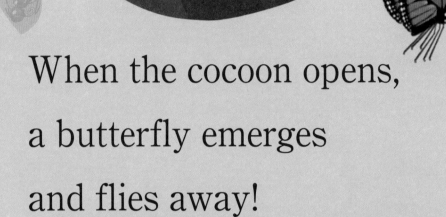

When the cocoon opens,
a butterfly emerges
and flies away!

egg

caterpillar

butterfly

pupa

Praying Mantis!

The praying mantis has
special legs to catch its prey.
When prey comes near,
the mantis grabs it.

A large praying mantis
can even catch
hummingbirds!
"I'm out
of here!"
Chris says.

Honeybee!

Honeybees are
hard workers.
They collect nectar
from flowers.
This is food for their hive.
Thousands of bees
live in a single hive!

Bees have to be careful.
Predators like the crab spider
hide in the flowers
to catch them.

Golden Orb Spider!

Many spiders make webs
to catch their prey.
The sticky webs are strong
and hard to see.

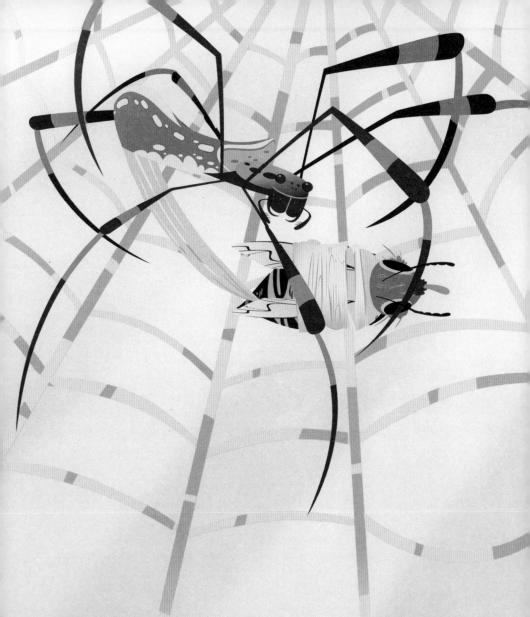

When an insect gets stuck
in the web, the spider kills it
and wraps it up to eat later!

"There are over one million kinds of insects and spiders!" Chris says. "We've got lots more insect adventuring to do!" Martin adds.

Go, Creature Powers!

Wild Predators

by Martin Kratt and Chris Kratt

Random House 🏠 New York

Predators can be strong,
fast, and smart.
They can have sharp teeth
and claws or other amazing
Creature Powers.

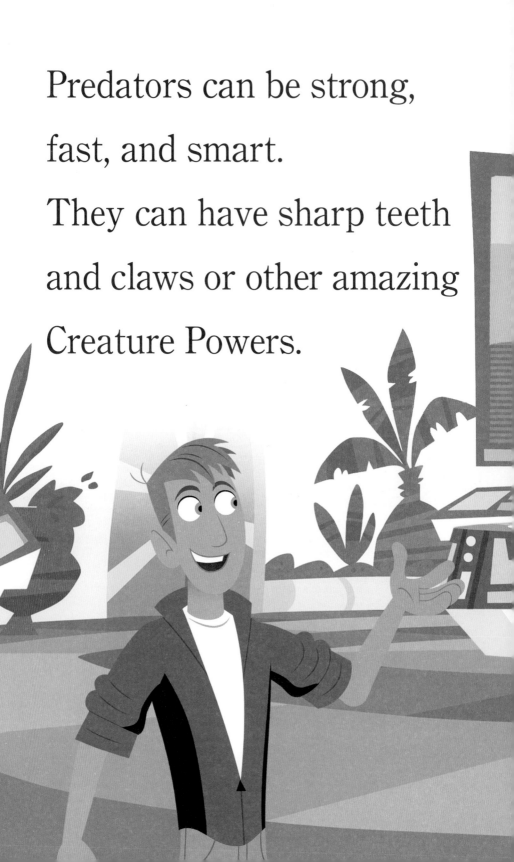

But what are predators?

Predators are animals
that catch and eat
other animals.

The animals that
predators catch
are called prey.

But catching prey
can be tricky. . . .

Get ready to activate
Predator Powers with us,
the Wild Kratts!

Jaguars!

Jaguars are big jungle cats that are powerful swimmers. These cats can catch caimans!

They can be black or spotted.

Ospreys!

Ospreys have big eyes

to spot fish in the water.

When an osprey

sees a fish,

the bird dives

and plucks the fish

out of the water

with sharp talons.

"My turn. Biggest fish wins!" says Chris.

Mouse Lemurs!

Not all predators look fierce.

The mouse lemur looks cute!

"My new fuzzy friend!"

says Martin.

Don't be fooled!

Mouse lemurs are fierce.

They can jump far and

grab insects and lizards

in their paws.

"Run!" the Kratts shout.

Fossas!

Fossas live and hunt
on the island
of Madagascar.
Fossas have incredible
climbing powers.

They can run down
a tree headfirst!
Their favorite prey
is lemurs.

Polar Bears!

Polar bears hunt on land and in the sea.

Their white fur hides them while they hunt in the snow.

This is called camouflage.

Polar bears are strong
swimmers.
They hunt seals and walrus
in the icy waters
of the Arctic Ocean!

Black-Footed Ferrets!

Black-footed ferrets are long, slim, and fast.

They run through tunnels
to catch their favorite prey—
prairie dogs!

Praying Mantis!

A praying mantis has
two long front legs
with spikes.
When a bug walks by,
the praying mantis
snatches it up!

"Let me try!" says Martin.

"Don't bug me, bro!"

Chris says.

Cheetahs!

Cheetahs are the fastest land predators. They chase speedy prey like gazelles.

Cheetahs can run seventy
miles per hour.
Cheetahs are long
and skinny,
which helps them sprint.

Wolves!

Wolves are also runners.
They can run
for a long time.

Wolves hunt in a pack.
They work together
to catch big animals,
such as moose.

Thorny Devils!

Ants are the thorny devil's favorite prey.

In fact, ants are the only thing this reptile eats!

A thorny devil
uses its sticky tongue
to pick up ants.
It can eat over a thousand
ants each day!

Roadrunners!

Roadrunners are the
fastest-running birds
in North America.
They chase and catch
lizards and other small
desert creatures.

These quick birds also hunt
venomous rattlesnakes.
"Too much tug-of-war
for me," says Martin.
"Time to activate
Roadrunner Powers!"

"Race you to our
next meal!" says Chris.
"You're on!" says Martin.
Go, Creature Powers!

Wild Reptiles

Snakes,

Crocodiles, Lizards,

and Turtles!

by Martin Kratt and Chris Kratt

Random House New York

Imagine if you could do what reptiles do.

You could crawl, climb,
or slither just like them.

But what are reptiles?

Most reptiles hatch from eggs.

Reptiles have scales.

Reptiles are cold-blooded.

That means they need the sun

to get warm.

Crocodiles and alligators,
lizards, snakes, and turtles
are all reptiles.

Let's learn more about them.

Activate Creature Powers!

Rattlesnakes!

A rattlesnake has special scales on its tail.

The scales are used
to make a rattling sound.
The sound is a warning
that the snake wants
to be left alone.

Rattlesnakes have long fangs.
They use their fangs
to catch food and
defend themselves.
Venom comes through
the fangs when they strike.

The venom is poisonous.

"Watch out!"

Martin warns a coyote.

Crocodiles!

The Nile crocodile is one of
the biggest reptiles!
It is not afraid of
the hippos and lions
that also use the river.

A Nile crocodile has
more than 60 teeth.
"Open wide!" says Chris.

A mother crocodile is gentle
with her babies.
She watches over them
and protects them.

She even carries them
carefully in her jaws.
"This is a fun way to travel,"
says Martin.

Draco Lizards!

A Draco lizard has wing-like structures that unfold from its sides to help it move through the air.

It can glide from tree to tree.

Jump! Glide! Land!

"Dracos make it look easy.

I need more practice,"

says Chris.

Basilisk Lizards!

Many reptiles swim.
Only one can run
on top of the water!

The basilisk lizard
has big webbed feet.
Its feet move so fast,
it can run across the water
without sinking.

"Wait for me!" shouts Chris.

Gila Monsters!

These lizards mostly
live underground.
They only come up
for sun, water, and food.

"Nice to get out
once in a while,"
says Martin.

Rock Pythons!

A python is a constricting
snake.
It wraps around its prey
and squeezes,
then swallows it whole!

Rock pythons live in holes on the African savannah. They eat gazelles and warthogs.

"Want me to untangle you now?" asks Martin.

Geckos!

Geckos are small lizards
with a big Creature Power.

A gecko has special toes that can hold on to almost any surface. Even glass!

Turtles!

There are more than 300 different kinds of turtles and tortoises— with one creature power in common: a shell!

It helps to protect them
when they are in danger.
The Tortuga is shaped
like a turtle.
It protects the
Wild Kratts.

Alligators!

Alligators are related
to crocodiles,
but they have wide snouts.
Crocodiles have pointy,
narrow snouts.

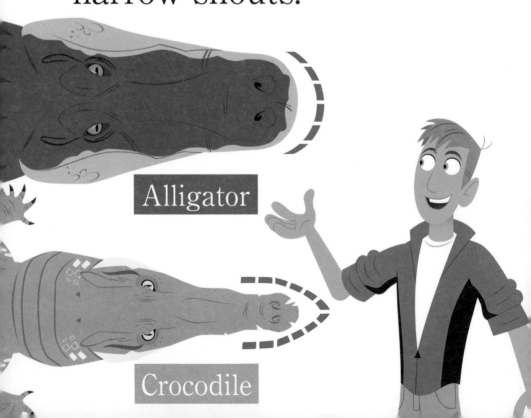

Alligator

Crocodile

Alligators are
grayish black.
Crocodiles are
brownish green.
Both creatures can grow
to be very big.

"Later, gator!" says Chris.

"In a while, crocodile!"

Martin replies.

Go, Creature Powers!

Wild Sea Creatures Sharks, Whales, and Dolphins!

by Martin Kratt and Chris Kratt

Random House 🏠 New York

What if you could do
what sea creatures do?
You could eat, swim,
and live underwater.

We are the Wild Kratts.
Get ready to activate
Creature Powers
and dive deep with us.

Tiger Sharks!

Tiger sharks have stripes on their sides.

Tiger sharks are predators.
A predator eats other
animals.
Tiger sharks like to eat
sea turtles.

Sea Turtles!

Sea turtles are reptiles. They have tough shells to protect them from harm.

"It is like a shield," Martin tells Chris.

Sperm Whales!

Sperm whales are
one of the biggest kinds
of whales.
A baby sperm whale
is very big, too.

Martin says, "Let's take
a deep breath
and get ready to dive!"

Sperm whales breathe air
but can dive very deep.
They can swim to
the bottom of the sea
in search of their
favorite food, squid.

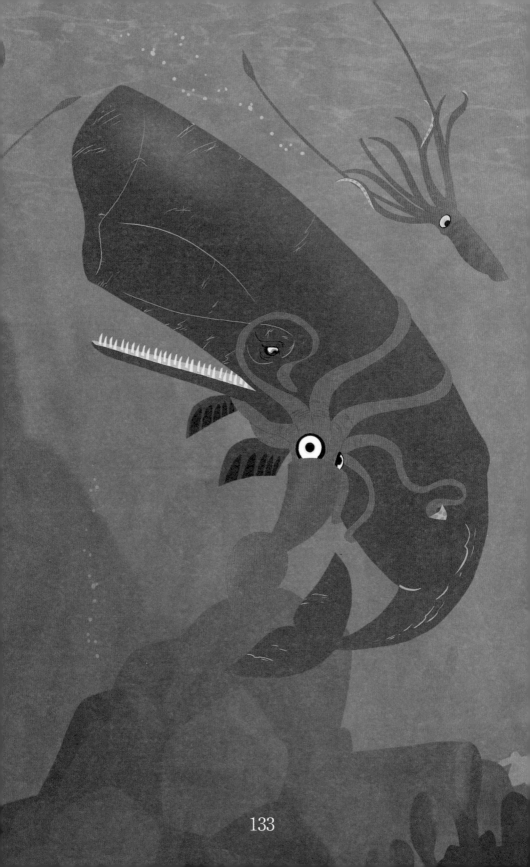

Colossal Squid!

Whales and squids
have big battles.
Squids fight with arms
and long tentacles.
But the whales usually
win and eat the squids!

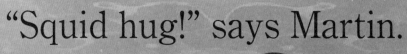

"Squid hug!" says Martin.

Blowfish!

Blowfish look like
ordinary fish.
Then they blow up!

They become round, spiny, and too big for predators to swallow.

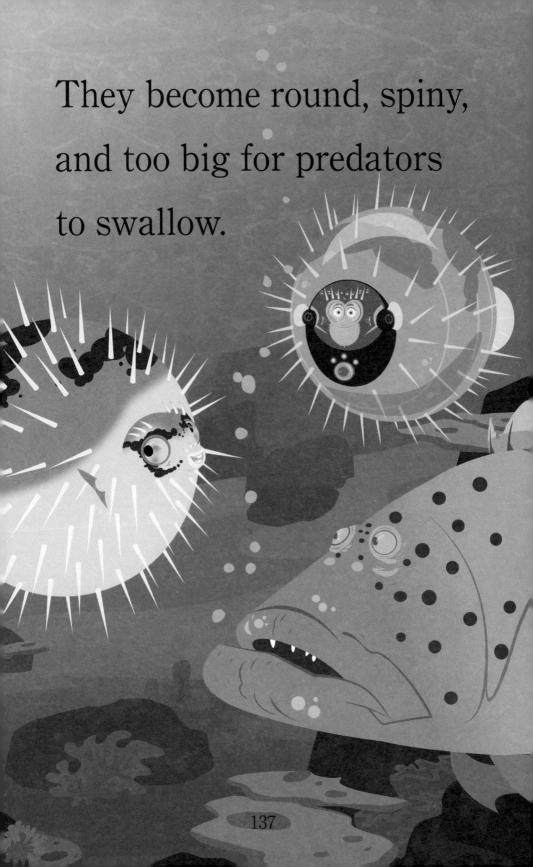

Yeti Crabs!

Yeti crabs live
deep in the dark sea.
These small crabs have "hairs"
on their legs and claws.
The hairs help them catch
little bits of food to eat.

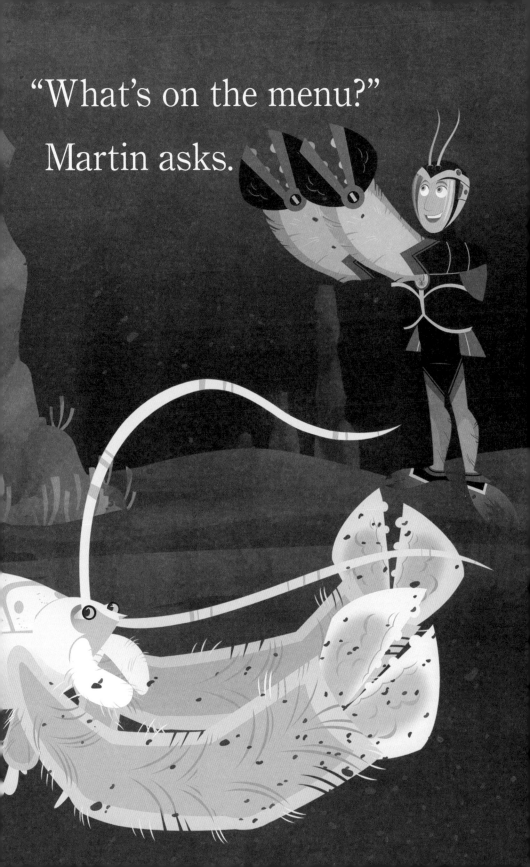

"What's on the menu?"
Martin asks.

Dolphins!

Dolphins are always
on the go.

Dolphins swim.

Dolphins jump.

Dolphins round up fish to eat.

And watch out for sharks!

Great White Sharks!

Great white sharks are
the biggest hunting sharks.
They have large, sharp teeth
and a keen sense of smell.
They hunt alone,
and they like to eat
dolphins!

Dolphins work together
to fight back.

Great white sharks
never stop swimming.
They live in oceans
around the world.

"Let's keep moving!"
Chris cheers.

Moray Eels!

Moray eels live in
rock and coral caves.
They are predators.
They eat fish.

This moray eel does not see
the frogfish that is hiding.
Do you?
Frogfish blend in
with their habitat.

Flying Fish!

Some fish swim fast.

Other fish hide.

And some fish fly to escape

from predators.

Flying fish use their fins

to glide into the air!

But that
doesn't mean
these fish
are safe!

"You got me, bro!"
says Martin.
Go, Creature Powers!

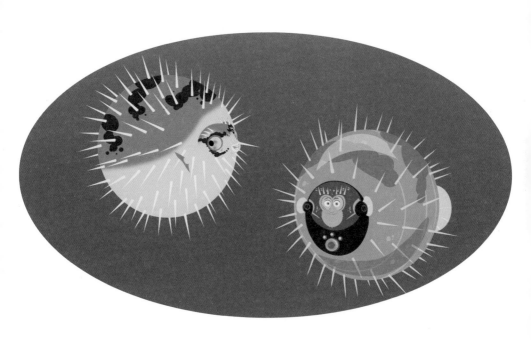

What is your favorite Wild Animal Baby? Why?

_____

_____

_____

What is your favorite Wild Insect or Spider? Why?

_____

_____

_____

What is your favorite Wild Predator? Why?

_____

_____

_____

What is your favorite Wild Reptile? Why?

_____

_____

_____

What is your favorite Wild Sea Creature? Why?

_____

_____

_____

About the Authors

Brothers **Chris Kratt** and **Martin Kratt** are zoologists by training who have built a family entertainment brand based on their enthusiasm for animals and their wild popularity with a family audience. Since founding their production company, Kratt Bros. Co., in 1993, they have created and executive-produced over 200 episodes of four successful television series: *Kratts' Creatures, Zoboomafoo with the Kratt Brothers, Kratt Bros. Be the Creature,* and *Wild Kratts.* They star in these programs as themselves and are directors, scriptwriters, authors, and wildlife cinematographers, ever in the pursuit of "creature adventure."